Where does a COWGIRL go Potty?

Written by Dawn Babb Prochovnic

Illustrated by Jacob Souva

WEST MARGIN PRESS

For Katia, who appreciates the importance of regular potty stops. —D.P.

For Natalia, my pardner in many silly adventures. —J.S.

Text © 2019 by Dawn Babb Prochovnic
Illustrations © 2019 by Jacob Souva

Edited by Michelle McCann

Library of Congress Control Number: 2019905575

ISBN 9781513262383 (hardbound)
ISBN 9781513262390 (e-book)

Printed in China
22 21 20 19 1 2 3 4 5

Published by West Margin Press®

WEST
MARGIN
PRESS

WestMarginPress.com

Proudly distributed by Ingram Publisher Services

WEST MARGIN PRESS
Publishing Director: Jennifer Newens
Marketing Manager: Angela Zbornik
Editor: Olivia Ngai
Design & Production: Rachel Lopez Metzger

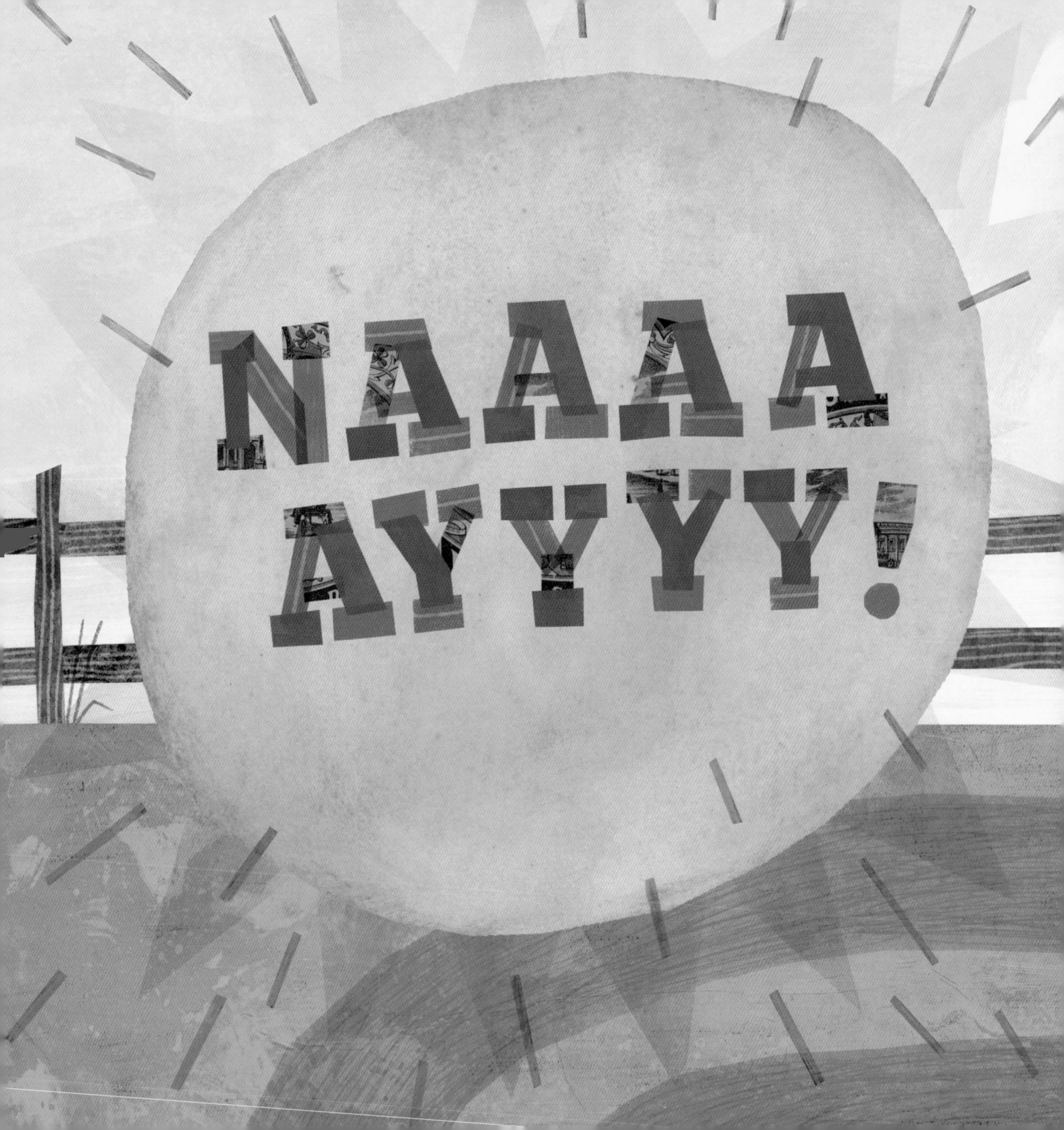
NAAAA
AYYYY!

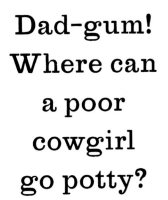

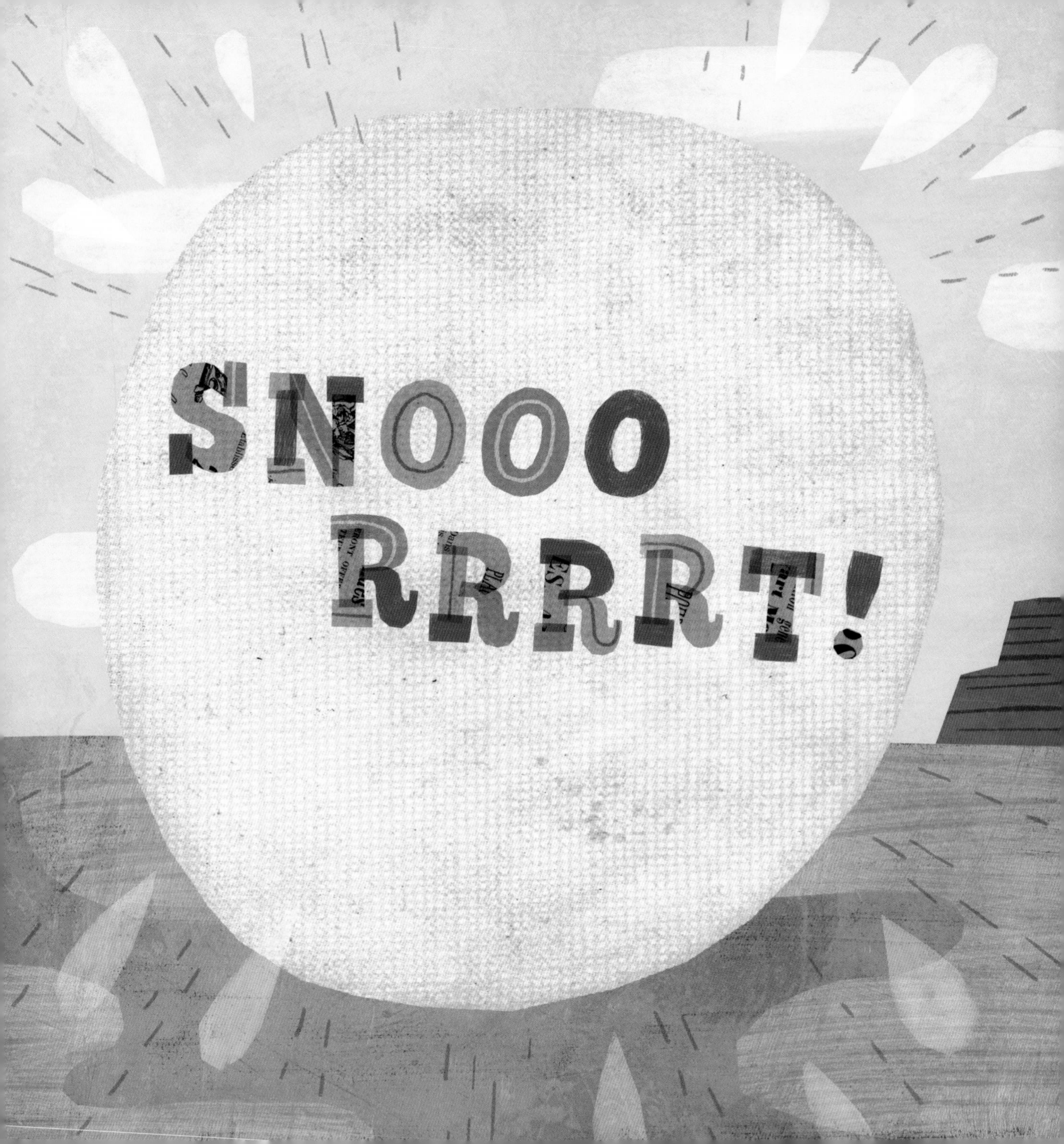
SNOOO
RRRRT!